RELAY RACE BREAKDOWN

BY JAKE MADDOX

Text by
THOMAS KINGSLEY TROUPE

Illustrations by
EDUARDO GARCIA

Jake Maddox books are published by Stone Arch Books
A Capstone Imprint
1710 Roe Crest Drive
North Mankato, Minnesota 56003
www.capstonepub.com

Library of Congress Cataloging-in-Publication Data

Maddox, Jake.
  Relay race breakdown / by Jake Maddox ; text by Thomas Kingsley Troupe ; illustrated by Eduardo Garcia.
       p. cm. -- (Jake Maddox sports story)
  Summary: Nick hates running, but his gym teacher thinks he is just the right person to fill in for the two-hundred-meter relay race, and will not give him a passing grade unless he tries--will Nick learn to run or let the team down?
  ISBN 978-1-4342-3289-2 (library binding) -- ISBN 978-1-4342-3903-7 (pbk.)
  1. Running races--Juvenile fiction. 2. Relay racing--Juvenile fiction. 3. Teamwork (Sports)--Juvenile fiction. 4. High schools--Juvenile fiction. [1. Racing--Fiction. 2. Teamwork (Sports)--Fiction. 3. High schools--Fiction. 4. Schools--Fiction.] I. Troupe, Thomas Kingsley. II. Garcia, Eduardo, 1970 Aug. 31- ill. III. Title. IV. Series.

  PZ7.M25643Rel 2012
  813.6--dc23

                                          2011032458

Graphic Designer: Russell Griesmer
Production Specialist: Michelle Biedscheid

Printed in the United States of America in Stevens Point, Wisconsin.
102011
006404WZS12

TABLE OF CONTENTS

CHAPTER 1

THE DEAL

Nick Reyes peered around the corner at the end of a long hallway at Central Junior High School. He looked left, then right. The coast was clear.

Nick sighed in relief. He was hiding out. In fact, he'd been hiding out all day, ever since his gym teacher, Mr. Swanson, had asked to talk to him after class. Nick was pretty sure he knew why. It was about his running. Or, more likely, lack of running.

Normally Nick liked gym well enough, but last month they'd done a cross-country unit. Nick hated running. He knew he was terrible at it. He always felt like the slowest kid in class. It was embarrassing.

Luckily, he only had gym once a week. He'd managed to get out of running with one excuse or another each time they ran. But he was out of excuses.

Nick had avoided Mr. Swanson all day. By now, he should have been out of the school and home free, but he'd forgotten a book in his locker.

Just get the book, and you're home free, Nick thought. He peered around the corner and got ready to make his move.

Just then, he heard footsteps behind him. "Hey there, Nick," a voice called. "I've been looking for you."

Nick turned around to see Mr. Swanson standing behind him, holding a clipboard. He didn't look happy.

Oh, no, Nick thought. *I almost made it.*

"I thought I asked you to stop in and talk to me after class," Mr. Swanson said. He tapped his clipboard with a pen. "We have a small problem. I don't have any kind of grade for you on the cross-country portion of the class."

Nick sighed. He knew Mr. Swanson had noticed.

"You didn't run the mile with the rest of the class," Mr. Swanson said. "In fact, I have you marked absent every time we ran. We never scheduled a make-up run."

Nick gulped. "You want me to run the mile?" he asked. "Right now?"

Mr. Swanson shook his head. "No, not right now," he said. "But you do need to make it up. I have an offer for you. Did you hear what happened to Ben Cribbage?"

"Yeah," Nick said. "Someone said he sprained his ankle last weekend."

Mr. Swanson nodded. "Ben was supposed to run in a relay race at the end of the month," he said. "Now the track team is short one runner."

"That's too bad," Nick said. When Mr. Swanson didn't say anything, it hit him. "Wait . . . you want me to run in Ben's place? Me?"

"I do," Mr. Swanson said. "The race is a 4-by-200-meter relay with three other guys. You'll only have to run 200 meters. That's only about an eighth of a mile."

Nick thought about it. He didn't like the idea, but running a whole mile by himself sounded worse.

"I'm not really a track guy," Nick said. "I'm not very good. I doubt the rest of the guys will want me on their team, especially if this is some big race."

Mr. Swanson folded his arms. "Run the race and I'll pass you, Nick," he said firmly. "Or you can do the mile. It's up to you."

Nick looked down at the floor. He knew he didn't have much of a choice. After a moment, he looked up and nodded.

"Okay," Nick said. "I'll do it."

"Great," Mr. Swanson replied. "The team has practice tomorrow after school. You can start then."

CHAPTER 2
MEET THE TEAM

The next day, Nick's classes dragged by. He couldn't stop thinking about what he'd gotten himself into. He hated running. And he really didn't want to run with a bunch of other guys from the track team. They'd be great. And he knew he'd be terrible.

At the end of the day, his friend Josh came up to his locker.

"You want to shoot some hoops after school?" Josh asked.

"I can't," Nick said as he shut his locker. "I'm have to practice for the relay race."

"How did you get sucked into that, dude?" Josh asked.

Nick sighed and explained the whole deal to his friend. "So basically I'm joining the relay team," he finished.

Josh shook his head and laughed. "You were tricked, Nick," he said. "If he has you practice with those guys after school every day, you'll end up running way more than a mile."

"Every day?" Nick repeated.

"Did you think you were just going jog a little bit and then go home until the big race?" Josh asked. "No way. You'll have to do all sorts of conditioning drills with them. Sprints, laps, you name it."

Nick felt his stomach sink. "Great," he muttered. "Just perfect."

* * *

"Hey," Mr. Swanson called as Nick walked outside. "There he is!"

Nick saw his gym teacher wave him over from the track surrounding the school's football field. Nearby, three other guys waited. They were all wearing running shorts and tank tops.

Since he didn't have a track uniform of his own, Nick wore his gym clothes from class.

I'd rather be anywhere but here, Nick thought. *They'll probably have me running all over the place.*

"Sorry I'm late," Nick muttered as he got closer.

"No worries," Mr. Swanson said. "I want to introduce you to the guys. They're all really glad you decided to join."

A smaller guy stepped forward to shake Nick's hand. "I'm Andy," the boy said. "I run first."

"I run when I have to," Nick said.

Mr. Swanson smiled. "Nick's new to relay races," he said. "We'll work with him and get him up to speed."

"We're just grateful to have a fourth runner," the guy in glasses next to Andy said. "I'm Tyler, by the way."

Nick nodded and waved.

"And last but not least," Mr. Swanson said, nudging the next guy with his elbow. The boy had shaggy hair that nearly covered his eyes.

"Hey, I'm Drew," he said. He shook his hair out of his face.

"Nice to meet you," Nick said. "Sorry to hear about Ben."

"We were, too," Andy said. He glanced over at his teammates. "Especially since Ben used to run anchor."

"Why does it matter what position Ben ran?" Nick asked. "Doesn't everyone have to run the same amount?"

"The guy who runs anchor, or the last leg, is usually the fastest on the team," Tyler explained. "The anchor is the one to cross the finish line with the baton. Ben used to really tear up his leg of the race when we needed him to."

"Wow," Nick said. "So Ben was, like, your most valuable player?"

"Definitely," Andy said. "We're not sure who's going to run in his place."

Nick nodded, but he still wondered why it was a big deal. Everyone had to run well for the team to win. Did it really matter who ran last?

"All right, guys," Mr. Swanson said. "Let's do some warm-up stretches to get started."

Nick shook his head. "I'm good," he lied. "I stretched in the locker room before."

"We always stretch as a team," Andy said. "Trust me, it'll help."

"A little more stretching won't hurt you," Mr. Swanson said. "It'll give me a chance to explain how the race will work."

Nick sighed. *Looks like there's no getting out of this*, he thought.

Nick sat down on the ground and copied the other runners' positions. He put both legs straight out in front of him and bent at the waist. Keeping his knees straight, Nick reached his fingers toward his toes. He could feel the stretch along the back of his legs in his hamstrings.

"So, Nick, like I said, we're running the 4-by-200-meter relay," Mr. Swanson explained. "Once around the track is 400 meters. That means you'll be running halfway around."

"Okay," Nick said, looking over at the track. It didn't look like it was that far, but he knew it would feel worse once he was running. He copied the new stretch the rest of the team was doing. He crossed his right leg over his left and twisted his body, stretching out his hip muscles.

Mr. Swanson pointed to a line at the midway mark on the track. "Andy will start there," he said, "and run around to the other side where he'll hand off the baton to . . ." Mr. Swanson hesitated. "We still need to figure out the new running order."

"I'll run second," Tyler offered. He stood up from the ground and jogged across the field to the opposite side of the track.

"Tyler will run back to the first line and pass it to you, Nick," Mr. Swanson said.

"I have to run anchor?" Drew grumbled. "Seriously?"

"This is just practice, Drew," Mr. Swanson reminded him. "We'll figure out who runs anchor once we see how Nick does."

Don't count on me, Nick thought. *You definitely don't want me running last.*

Drew sighed. Nick could tell he wasn't happy about having to run anchor. But Drew stood up and crossed the field to stand near Tyler.

Mr. Swanson handed the baton to Andy. The baton looked like a small silver stick of dynamite without the fuse.

"Make sure you have a good handoff," he told Nick. "That's one of the most important parts of a relay race. If the baton falls into another runner's lane, we're disqualified."

"Does that happen?" Nick asked. *I don't want to be the one to drop the baton and get us disqualified*, he thought nervously.

"Sometimes," Andy said. "You get so focused on running, and the next thing you know, the baton's on the ground."

"Let's have you two get into position on this side," Mr. Swanson said. He turned to Nick. "See that line about four steps behind you? When you see Tyler hit that mark, start running to receive the handoff. That way you'll be in the passing zone."

Nick looked confused. "What's the passing zone?" he asked.

"It's the area you have to pass the baton in," Mr. Swanson explained. "You have to do it in that 20-meter space, or the team is disqualified. Make sure you're looking straight ahead, and hold your right hand straight out behind you at hip height. As soon as you feel the baton in your hand, start running as fast as you can."

Great, Nick thought. *One more thing for me to mess up.*

Once they were all in position around the track, Mr. Swanson stepped off to the side of the track near Nick and Andy. He pulled out a starting gun and shot it to signal the start.

Andy took off with the baton in his hand. He ran so fast, his legs were a blur. It looked like Andy was flying. In no time, Andy was rounding the turn to where Tyler stood waiting. As Andy got closer, Tyler started jogging and reached behind him. In no time, the baton was in his hand, and Tyler ran with it.

"Get ready," Mr. Swanson called from the sidelines. "Start running like Tyler did, and watch for him to come around the curve."

Nick didn't feel ready at all, but he started jogging. He heard Tyler's feet thundering along the track. Tyler ran closer and closer.

"Here it comes," Mr. Swanson shouted. "Watch for the handoff!"

Nick ran. He could hear Tyler close behind him.

"Stick," Tyler shouted. A moment later, the metal baton slapped Nick's palm.

But before Nick could close his hand, the baton dropped to the ground. It bounced across three lanes.

Mr. Swanson blew his whistle. "You're disqualified," he said.

Great, Nick thought. *I'm even worse than I thought.*

CHAPTER 3
A WAY OUT

Mr. Swanson wasn't upset that Nick dropped the baton, but he made him run his 200 meters anyway. It hadn't ended there. For the rest of practice they'd done conditioning work: sprints, lunges, and squats. Plus laps — lots and lots of laps.

"See you tomorrow, Nick," Mr. Swanson said. "Don't forget, we have practice every day until the meet."

Just like Josh warned me, Nick thought.

When Nick got home, he was drenched with sweat and exhausted. He dropped his backpack in the entryway.

"Wow," his mom said. "What happened to you?"

"I got roped into being on the track team," Nick mumbled as he went upstairs.

Nick headed to the bathroom and turned on the shower. *How can people actually like running?* he thought. *Every day?*

Nick leaned against the wall while he waited for the water to warm up. Even though Coach had made them stretch at the beginning and end of practice, every muscle in his body ached. His clothes were soaked. He had blisters on his feet from where his running shoes had rubbed, and his legs felt like rubber.

To make matters worse, he'd fumbled the handoff repeatedly. He'd felt like he was slowing the entire team down during practice.

It's official, Nick thought. *Running is the worst. And I'm the worst at it.*

Nick opened the cabinet and rooted through the basket his mom kept the first aid stuff in. Behind the box of bandages, Nick noticed the brown roll of fabric held together with a small silver clasp.

An ACE bandage. His mom had twisted her ankle years ago in the garden, and she'd used it to wrap up her swollen foot.

Ben can't race because he sprained his ankle, Nick thought. *If the team thinks I'm injured, that means I can't run either. They'll probably be relieved. I'm slowing everyone else down anyway.*

Nick smiled. He might have found a way to get out of running after all.

* * *

The next morning at school, Nick knocked on Mr. Swanson's office door. Nick balanced carefully himself on the crutches and made sure to keep his bandaged foot up. After a moment, the door opened.

"Nick," Mr. Swanson said, looking upset. "What happened?"

"I decided to run some more after practice last night," Nick said, feeling his neck grow hot. *I'm a terrible liar*, he thought. "I ran around a corner, and my shoe caught a patch of sand. I slipped and twisted my ankle pretty bad."

"This is terrible," Mr. Swanson said. "The guys are going to be crushed."

"Really?" Nick asked. "I wasn't all that good last night."

"That's not true," Mr. Swanson replied. "You did a good job for your first practice. It just takes a while to get the handoff down. And you had some decent running times. 30 seconds for 200 meters is pretty good for a beginner." He let out a deep sigh. He shook his head and gazed down at Nick's bandaged foot. "I'll let them know."

"Tell them I'm sorry," Nick said.

Mr. Swanson nodded. "Take care of that ankle," he added.

Nick felt a wave of guilt wash over him. *I'll get over it*, he thought. *It's worth it to not have to run anymore.* He turned around on his mom's crutches and winced. They hurt his armpits.

"Before I forget," Mr. Swanson called. "I'll need a doctor's note, too, okay? We have to have one for these kinds of things."

"Oh," Nick said. "I don't have it with me."

"No worries," Mr. Swanson said. "Just bring it tomorrow."

CHAPTER 4
MOM'S ADVICE

By the time Nick got home from school, his armpits ached from rubbing on the crutches all day. Even though his ankle was fine, he'd had to keep pretending his ankle was sprained. Once he was inside, he headed into his room. He quickly hid the crutches in his closet.

Now I'm really stuck, Nick thought as he flopped down onto his bed. *What have I gotten myself into?*

Nick sat down at his desk. He found a piece of paper and tried to come up with a believable doctor's note.

TO NICK'S GYM TEACHER: NICK HAS A SPRAINED ANKLE AND CAN'T RUN.

THANKS, DR. STEPHENS

Nick read the note out loud and crumpled it up. No one would believe that. He tried different versions, but each one sounded worse than the last. The writing looked wrong, and the note didn't even have a doctor's signature.

Nick thought about the other guys on the team. They were probably practicing without him right now. Nick wondered if they were upset that he wasn't there. He felt bad, but he didn't know what else to do. He absolutely hated running.

"Nick?" his mom called. "Are you home?" He heard footsteps on the stairs, and then his mom opened the door. "I didn't hear you come in," she said.

"I'm here," Nick said. "I guess I was just extra quiet."

"What happened to your ankle?" his mom asked, coming into the room. She pointed at the brown ACE bandage, which was still wrapped around his ankle. "Did you get hurt during track practice?"

Nick took a deep breath. Then he explained how he'd faked his injury to get out of running the relay race.

"I don't know what to do," Nick said. "If I tell Mr. Swanson the truth, he's going to be so mad at me. But if I don't, he'll know I was faking it when I don't have a note. I'm stuck."

Nick's mom sat down in the chair in front of his desk. "What do you think you should do?" she asked.

"Could we move to a new town?" Nick suggested. "Maybe I could go to a different school?"

Mom shook her head and smiled.

Nick sighed. "I'll tell the truth," he said.

His mom nodded, but then she raised her eyebrows. "That's a start," she said. "But Mr. Swanson isn't the only one you need to come clean with."

Nick nodded. "Yeah," he said. "You're right. The guys on the relay team are going to think I'm the worst."

"Maybe not," Mom said. "Not if you make it up to them."

CHAPTER 5

COMING CLEAN

The next day, Nick ran into Mr. Swanson on his way to gym class.

"Hey, Nick," Mr. Swanson said. "No more crutches! Is your ankle feeling better?"

"Yeah," Nick said. "Actually, I need to talk to you about that." Nick took a deep breath. "I made up the story about twisting my ankle. I didn't hurt it. It's fine."

Mr. Swanson folded his arms and stared at Nick expectantly.

"I'm really sorry," Nick said. "It was dumb. You gave me another chance, and I blew it."

Mr. Swanson was quiet for a minute. "Why did you do it?" he asked. "Why put up such a huge fight about running?"

Nick sighed. "I hate running," he said. "I've never liked it. I'm not good at it. It's not nearly as fun as basketball or football. I get so tired and sweaty and out of breath. And I'm always the slowest runner."

Nick paused for a moment. "Running with three other guys who love it made it even worse," he said. "I was embarrassed. I figured they'd be grateful they didn't have me slowing the whole team down."

"Well, first of all, I accept your apology," Mr. Swanson said.

"Thanks," Nick responded. He was afraid he'd end up in huge trouble for lying in the first place.

"But it doesn't matter if you don't like to run," Mr. Swanson said. "Running is part of the class and a significant portion of your grade. And you're not bad it. Running takes practice, just like any other sport. That's the only way you'll get faster."

"I guess," Nick said.

"And finally," Mr. Swanson continued, "you need to apologize to the guys on the team. They were really upset about losing you. They're worried about this next race."

"I plan on apologizing," Nick said. He meant it. "Can I do it at practice tonight?"

"I thought you didn't want to run with them," Mr. Swanson said.

"I need to give it another try," Nick said. "I just hope they'll take me back."

* * *

Nick met the rest of the runners at the track after school. Andy was the first to talk after Nick explained what he'd done.

"So you faked the whole thing?" Andy asked. He crossed his arms angrily. "Who does that?"

"Someone who hates running," Nick admitted. "But I want to give it another try. For real this time. If you guys will give me another chance, that is."

"I don't know," Tyler said. "What if you decide to quit or come up with another fake injury? Then we're really in trouble."

Nick shook his head. "Not going to happen," he said. "I promise."

Everyone looked at Drew. He was the only one who hadn't said anything. He brushed his hair out of his face and shrugged.

"Look at it this way," Drew said finally. "He came clean, didn't he? That's got to count for something."

The other guys nodded and looked to Mr. Swanson. The gym teacher put up his hands and took a step back.

"It's up to you guys," Mr. Swanson said. "This is your team."

Andy was quiet for a minute. Then he smiled. "All right," he said. "Welcome back to the team, Nick."

"Thanks guys," Nick said. "I won't let you down . . . again."

CHAPTER 6

HIT THE GROUND RUNNING

The runners quickly got down to business.

"I'll bet you were pretty sore after your first practice," Tyler said, grinning. He pulled his knee up to his chest and held it there.

"Yeah," Nick admitted. "I felt like I got hit by a truck."

"Stretching, man," Tyler said. "Always stretch before you run."

"You won't stop being sore right away," Drew added. He was on the ground with one leg tucked underneath him. He leaned over his outstretched leg and grabbed his foot. "But stretching makes it less horrible."

Less horrible, Nick thought. *This is sounding better all the time.*

Nick sat down on the grass and had the guys show him different ways to stretch. It worried him that even stretching made him sore. He wondered again what he'd gotten himself into.

Even so, Nick kept quiet. He'd made a promise, and he was going to keep it. After several minutes, the team was ready to run.

"Here's what we'll do, Nick," Mr. Swanson said. "To get started, I want you to run an entire lap, as fast as you can."

Nick eyed the track around the football field. It looked even longer than it did a couple of days ago. "I thought I just needed to run half a lap for the race," he said.

"True," Mr. Swanson said. "But if you run more during practice, doing 200 meters during the race will seem like nothing."

"I don't know about that," Nick said.

"Trust me," Mr. Swanson said. "Get to the starting line, and when I blow the whistle, run as fast as you can."

"Here," Andy said. He slapped the baton into Nick's hand. "You'll need to get used to carrying the baton when you're tearing around the track."

Nick approached the starting line and cleared his mind. All that mattered was getting around the track.

"Don't drop the baton," Tyler shouted.

Also, don't drop the baton, Nick thought.

The whistle blew, and Nick took off running as fast as he could.

Nick wanted to stop after just a few seconds. He was already out of breath. But he pushed on. He pumped his arms and tried to lengthen his strides. From the middle of the field, he heard the other guys yelling.

I'm going as fast as I can, Nick thought. It took him a moment to realize they were cheering.

Nick rounded the first bend. Sweat streamed from his hair and dribbled into his eyes. Nick wiped it away and pushed himself even more. A long straightaway was ahead, and before he knew it, he was halfway done.

Almost there, Nick thought. He focused on the end of the track.

As he rounded the last bend, Nick's legs felt like jelly. He was gasping for breath. Mr. Swanson shouted too, looking at his stopwatch.

Great, Nick thought as he crossed the finish line. *He's timing me!* When he slowed to a stop, the other guys clapped.

"Oh, man," Nick said, panting. He bent over and tried to catch his breath. "That was awful." He tossed the baton to Tyler and groaned.

"Not bad," Mr. Swanson said. "You did that in just over a minute. For a guy who doesn't like to run, you didn't do half bad."

Doesn't feel like I did half good, either, Nick thought.

CHAPTER 7
CHANGING IT UP

Running was hard, but Nick stuck with it. He showed up for every practice. Running laps over and over again seemed to be getting a bit easier. He wasn't as out of breath as he'd been the first time.

I've definitely run more than a mile, Nick thought while they practiced handing off the baton. He'd gotten better at the handoff. He even yelled "Stick!" to Tyler when he ran second during a practice.

It still felt strange to be part of a running team, but Nick actually enjoyed it. He still didn't totally love running, but he liked working with his new friends.

Even on weekends when they didn't have practice, Nick ran at the school track. The race was getting closer, and he wanted to practice as much as possible ahead of time. It was one thing to run in front of the guys and his coach. But there would be a lot of people watching at the race.

Nick cut a piece from an old wooden broom to use as a baton so he could practice running with it. He even started timing himself. He was getting a little faster each time. His time for a 200-meter run was down to 27 seconds.

At least I won't be the slowest guy there, Nick thought. *I hope.*

* * *

After all of the stretching and running and practicing, the Saturday of the big relay race finally arrived. Nick's mom dropped him off at the school for the meet. He headed to the track and nervously joined the rest of his team. Mr. Swanson stood in the center of the group. Everyone looked tense.

"What's going on?" Nick asked.

"I don't want to do it anymore," Drew said as Nick walked up. "I'm not up for it."

For a moment, Nick thought Drew didn't want to run at all. If that was the case, they were finished.

"Drew was supposed to run anchor," Andy explained, looking upset. "And now he doesn't want to."

Nick sighed. He could understand why Drew was freaking out. The anchor was crucial to the race.

"Well, why don't you run it?" Nick asked, looking at Andy.

"Me?" Andy exclaimed. "I run first! I always run first. It's tradition!"

Nick turned to Tyler.

"Don't look at me," Tyler said. "I'm happy running third. I just won't have someone to hand the baton to now."

"Well, someone has to run last," Nick said. "Otherwise all of this practice and running around was for nothing!"

The group was quiet for a moment. Finally, Drew spoke up. "Why don't you run anchor, Nick?" he suggested.

Nick felt like someone punched him in the stomach. "Me?" he asked. "Are you serious? I'm the worst runner in the group!"

"I wouldn't say that," Drew replied.

"Neither would I," Tyler added.

Nick turned to Mr. Swanson for help, but the gym teacher just stood back and smiled. "It's your call, Nick," he said. "And for the record, you're a pretty good runner."

Pretty good doesn't win races, Nick thought. He could feel the guys on his team watching him. They waited for Nick to say something.

"Fine," Nick said. "I'll do it."

CHAPTER 8
A HARD SAVE

"Are you nervous?" Drew asked Nick as they took their positions on the opposite side of the track. Runners from other schools were lining up in their lanes too.

"Yeah," Nick admitted. "I was supposed to run second, but now I'm taking your spot. Thanks for nothing."

Drew shook his hair out of his eyes and laughed. "You'll be fine," he said. "Besides, anchor was never my spot. It was Ben's."

Nick took a deep breath and stood off to the side while the second-leg runners found their spots on the track. He knew his mom was somewhere in the crowd, but he couldn't see her from where he was standing. Nick looked across the track and saw Andy getting into position to run.

It won't be long now, Nick thought.

Within moments, the starter pistol fired. The runners leaped off the starting line. Andy got a fast start. By the time they rounded the first corner, he was in the middle of the pack. Andy overtook one of the guys as he headed into the straightaway.

Drew started running a little as Andy approached. As Andy got closer, Drew put his hand out to grab the baton.

"Stick!" Andy shouted. He slapped the baton into Drew's hand. Drew grabbed it and took off at full speed. A perfect handoff.

As Nick watched, one of the runners from another team flew around the curve. He had a solid lead over the rest of the group. Drew was in third place out of six, but gaining fast. In a matter of moments, their team had made up some ground.

Jeez, he's fast, Nick thought. He watched as the lead runner handed the baton off to his teammate. A moment later, Drew passed his baton to Tyler.

Nick got into position on the track and watched out of the corner of his eye as Tyler passed the third-place runner. Tyler was fast, which made Nick wonder why he wasn't running anchor instead of him.

Tyler rounded the last corner, but he couldn't pass the other two runners. As they got closer, Nick watched the runner in first place. In moments, the other team had passed the baton.

Nick started running as Tyler got closer. He put his hand out behind him at hip level and looked forward like he'd been taught.

"Stick!" Tyler shouted. He swung the baton down and hit Nick on the wrist instead of the hand. To Nick's horror, the baton bounced off of his arm and tumbled to the ground.

"No!" he heard Tyler yell.

Everything seemed to move in slow motion as Nick watched the baton fall. He knew that if it crossed the line and landed in another runner's lane, they were all disqualified.

Without thinking, Nick dove for the baton.

His knees struck the track hard. Small, sharp rocks dug into his skin. He ignored the pain and reached for the bouncing metal tube. Just as the baton was about to cross into another lane, Nick wrapped his hand around it. He barely managed to stay in the narrow lane.

Two runners flew past him.

"You're still in it, Nick," Tyler shouted. "Run!"

CHAPTER 9

THE FINAL PUSH

Get up, get up, Nick thought. He could hear the runner in last place closing in on him. With the baton in his hand, Nick pushed himself to his feet and ran.

Any ground Andy and Tyler had gained was gone. Nick knew that he had to run faster than he ever had before. His knees hurt with every stride, but he pushed on.

Nick heard people in the stands cheering. That made him run even faster.

His feet pounded along the track as he fought to make up lost ground. Both of his knees felt shredded. When he glanced down, he saw that they were bleeding.

Keep going, Nick told himself. *You can bandage them later.*

He raced past the guy in fourth place. A moment later, Nick passed the third-place runner as he barreled into the bend. Coming out of the turn, Nick was in third.

Once he hit the straightaway, Nick pumped his arms even harder. The back of the runner in front of him was getting closer.

Just finish strong, Nick thought. His lungs burned and sweat ran down his face. His knees stung where he'd fallen on them, and he wondered how scraped up they were. He didn't dare look. He had a race to finish.

"Go, Nick!" He heard Mr. Swanson shout from the sidelines. "You're almost there!"

It was true. In a matter of seconds, he would cross the finish line, and the race would be over. If only the handoff had been better! If only he hadn't dropped the baton!

Nick passed the runner in second place. He was startled to find himself on the heels of the lead runner. The crowd went crazy as they both drew closer to the finish line.

Come on, Nick thought as he pushed himself harder. But the other runner crossed the line a second before he did.

And just like that, it was over.

* * *

Nick slowed to a stop as his teammates ran over to him and looked down. He knew they'd be disappointed. He'd blown the race.

"Dude!" Drew shouted. "I knew we made the right choice switching you up!"

Nick looked up, surprised to see smiles on the faces of his teammates. Even Mr. Swanson was smiling.

"Great run, Nick," Mr. Swanson said. "That was an awesome recovery."

"Are you serious?" Nick asked. "I fumbled the baton and almost got us disqualified."

"That was my fault," Tyler said. "I was worn out, and my aim was off. I hit your arm, not your hand."

"With the way you ran, we could have won if the handoff had been better," Andy said.

"Second place is fine by me," Tyler said. "We'll get them next time."

"Next time?" Nick asked, a little confused.

"Yeah. We have another race in a week," Andy said.

Mr. Swanson laughed. "Slow down, guys," he said. "Nick just needed to run this one race to pass."

Nick was quiet for a moment. He was sweaty, his knees were bloody, and his heart was racing. But he'd actually had fun.

Maybe I don't hate running as much as I thought, Nick thought. *Besides, being on the team is pretty fun.* He grinned at his teammates.

"Yeah, I'll run another race," Nick said. He looked at Mr. Swanson. "Besides, I could use the extra credit."

About the Author

Thomas Kingsley Troupe writes, makes movies, and works as a firefighter/EMT. He's written many books for kids, including *Legend of the Vampire* and *Mountain Bike Hero*, and has two boys of his own. He likes zombies, bacon, orange Popsicles, and reading stories to his kids. Thomas currently lives in Woodbury, Minnesota, with his super-cool family.

About the Illustrator

Eduardo Garcia has illustrated for magazines around the world, including ones in Italy, France, United States, and Mexico. Eduardo loves working for publishers like Marvel Comics, Stone Arch Books, Idea + Design Works, and BOOM! Studios. Eduardo has illustrated many great characters like Speed Racer, the Spiderman family, Kade, and others. Eduardo is married to his beloved wife, Nancy M. Parrazales. They have one son, the amazing Sebastian Inaki, and an astonishing dog named Tomas.

GLOSSARY

baton (buh-TON)—a short stick passed from one runner to another in a relay race

crucial (KROO-shuhl)—extremely important

disqualified (diss-KWOL-uh-fyed)—banned from taking part in an activity, often because a rule has been broked

guilt (GILT)—a feeling of shame or remorse for having done something wrong

injury (IN-juh-ree)—damage or harm

relay (REE-lay)—a team race in which members of the team take turns running and passing a baton from one runner to the next

significant (sig-NIF-uh-kuhnt)—important or meaning a great deal

sprint (SPRINT)—a very fast race run over a short distance

tense (TENSS)—nervous or worried

DISCUSSION QUESTIONS

1. All the members of a relay team have to work together for the team to win. Have you ever been on a team? What kind? Talk about what it means to be part of a team.

2. Nick hates running, but in order to pass gym class he has to do it. Talk about something you don't like doing but have to do anyway.

3. Nick tried to lie to get out of joining the relay team. Talk about some other ways he could have dealt with his problem instead of lying.

WRITING PROMPTS

1. After finding out that Nick lied, his teammates were reluctant to let him back on the team. Write about how you would have felt if you were a member of the relay race team.

2. Nick was surprised when his teammates weren't upset about not winning the race. Write about a time someone reacted differently than you expected.

3. Do you think Nick will stick with the relay team now that he's discovered he likes being part of the team? Write a chapter that continues this story.

OLYMPIC RUNNING

The Olympic Games include five sprint and relay race events for both men and women, including two standard relay races. These are the 4x100-meter relay race and the 4x400-meter relay race.

Relay race teams are made up of four sprinters, each of whom runs one 400-meter lap. Here's a breakdown of the different events in the Summer Olympics:

- ▶ **100-METER DASH** — This race is run on a straightaway. All runners must remain in their lanes for the entire race.

- ▶ **200-METER DASH** — Just as in the 100-meter dash, runners must remain in their lanes for the length of the race. However, runners' starts are staggered to account for the curved track.

- **400-METER DASH** — The 400-meter dash is the same as the 200-meter dash, just longer. Runners must remain in their lanes for the length of the race. However, runners' starts are staggered to account for the curved track.

- **4 X 100-METER RELAY** — All runners in the relay race must remain in their lanes, and starts are staggered to make up for the curved track. Runners pass the baton to the next racer within a 20-meter passing zone.

- **4 X 400-METER RELAY** — In this relay race, only the first runner stays in the same lane for a full lap. After being given the baton, the second runner may leave the lane after the first turn. The third and fourth runners' lanes are assigned based on the position of the team's previous runner. Runners must hand off the baton within a 20-meter passing zone.